The
St. Patrick's Day
Shamrock
Mystery

D0951566

Marion M. Markham
Illustrated by Karen A. Jerome

Houghton Mifflin Company
Boston

Library of Congress Cataloging-in-Publication Data

Markham, Marion M.
  The St. Patrick's Day shamrock mystery / by Marion M. Markham ;
illustrated by Karen A. Jerome.
      p.   cm.
  Summary: On Saint Patrick's Day, the twin Dixon sleuths become
involved in a mystery unfolding right next door.
  ISBN 0-395-72137-7
  [1. Twins—Fiction.   2. Saint Patrick's Day—Fiction.   3. Mystery and
detective stories.]   I. Jerome, Karen A., ill.   II. Title.
PZ7.M33946St   1995   94-36716
[Fic]—dc20   CIP
                          AC

Printed in the United States of America

Reprinted by arrangement with Houghton Mifflin Company.
10 9 8 7 6 5 4 3 2 1

Contents

1

The Scientific Detective Club

Usually the Dixon twins didn't dress alike. To-day, however, they both wore green sweaters. On St. Patrick's Day it seemed natural to wear green, whether you were Irish or not.

At Springvale Airport the twins watched a large jetliner taxi for a takeoff. Kate liked to watch planes land and take off. She hoped that someday she would get to see all the instruments in a plane's cockpit. Science must have a lot to do with making a plane fly, Kate thought, and she liked science.

Mickey was more interested in mysteries. She liked to imagine that one of the people getting on or off an airplane was a spy with a coded message in his pocket. None of the people who got on this airplane had looked suspicious, except perhaps Horace Wink, whose red wool scarf flapped behind him. Mickey knew that Horace wasn't a spy. He was just the father of their next door neighbor, Miss Wink.

Amanda Wink also watched the jet, which was carrying her parents back home to Florida. She sniffed back tears as the plane lifted off from the long runway.

After the noise of jet engines faded, Mrs. Dixon said, "Would you like to do something today, Amanda — go shopping, perhaps?"

"No, thank you," Miss Wink said. "I had better go straight home. The kittens, you know."

This morning Horace had brought his daughter two kittens, telling her, "Now you won't be lonely after we're gone." One was reddish-tan with a white stomach. The other, a small gray kitten, had black lines above its nose.

Mr. Wink had picked up the gray kitten by the loose fur at the back of its neck. "This is Kilkenny. I took him because of the W on his forehead."

The black lines had looked like an M to Kate.

Horace winked. "Of course, the W is upside

down," he had said. "You can't expect a kitten to know how to spell Wink."

"What's the other kitten's name?" Kate had asked.

"Cork. Today being St. Patrick's Day, I named them after counties in Ireland."

Mickey thought it would have been better to let Miss Wink name the kittens herself, but Horace always did things his own way.

Now, as the airplane faded into a tiny speck in the sky, Mrs. Dixon said, "We better hurry or we'll get stuck behind the St. Patrick's Day Parade."

Hurry they did. Miss Wink might be anxious to get home to the kittens, but Mickey and Kate wanted to get back to their new clubhouse.

The clubhouse was really a shed in Miss Wink's back yard. The twins could see it from the rear porch of the apartment where they lived. Years ago, Horace, an inventor, had his workroom in the shed. Now, though, it was the home of the Scientific Detective Club. Horace had even painted the club name on a sign over the shed door. In smaller letters below the club name, he had printed in red, "Members Only."

Mickey had made him add that. "This club is just for Kate and me," she had said. "No one else."

Now, on the drive from the airport, Mickey took out a small notepad and made a list of things needed for a detective club.

So far she had six items:

Flashlight
Tape measure
Plastic sandwich bags for collecting clues
Cellophane tape to pick up fingerprints
Walkie-talkie (for birthday — me)
Small camera (birthday — get Kate to ask for)

"We really ought to have a magnifying glass to look at fingerprints," Mickey said.

"I can leave mine in the clubhouse," Kate offered. She used the magnifier to look at insects and moss. And she knew that it could be useful in looking for clues.

Mickey said, "Your microscope would also be handy."

"Only if we keep it in a plastic bag," Kate said. "The shed is damp and I don't want it to get rusty."

Mickey added a magnifying glass and a microscope to her list.

2

The Unknown Painter

As they turned the corner onto the street where they lived, the twins saw a big van. It was parked in front of their apartment house.

"I wonder who's moving," Kate said.

Mickey didn't say anything. She was adding "Book about codes" to her list.

As Mrs. Dixon backed into a space ahead of the van, Miss Wink gasped.

When the twins looked at her house, they forgot about moving vans and code books — someone had drawn a bright green shamrock on Miss Wink's front door.

Mrs. Dixon said, "How awful."

"My father just painted that door," Miss Wink wailed. "Now it's ruined."

"We'll help you repaint," Kate said.

"After we find out who did it," Mickey said. She jumped out of the car and ran up the steps. From the porch she said, "Don't touch anything."

"She wants to look for clues," Kate explained.

Everyone stared at the door.

"This was done by a very short person," Mickey said.

"How do you know?" her mother asked.

"It's a simple deduction. The green shamrock is only halfway up the door. See?" Mickey bent over and put out her hand. "I would have to stoop way down to paint it."

"A leprechaun!" Miss Wink exclaimed. She sometimes got strange ideas. Kate knew she would not have had this idea if it weren't St. Patrick's Day.

"There's no such thing as a leprechaun," she said. "It's a scientific fact."

"Then who?"

Mickey straightened up. "The Detective Club will uncover the villain," she said loudly.

"The *Scientific* Detective Club," Kate added. She knelt and studied the shamrock. In places the paint was shiny. Other spots were dull. She licked her finger and rubbed it across the green. It smeared.

"Poster paint," she said. "This will come off with water."

"Our first clue," Mickey said.

"Can we go in now?" Miss Wink asked. She fumbled in her purse for her key.

Before she could unlock the door, Mickey pushed against it. The door swung open.

"I saw it move when Kate streaked the paint," she explained.

Mrs. Dixon said, "Amanda, didn't you lock your house when we left for the airport?"

Miss Wink sighed. "I don't remember. There was so much confusion. My father was hurrying my mother. I was trying to wrap up a jar of my homemade quince jam for them. Kilkenny and Cork were getting underfoot. I finally had to shut the kittens in the basement. I guess I forgot about the door."

Mickey said, "Come on. Let's look for more clues." She went in.

"I'm almost afraid to see what they did to my house," Miss Wink said, although she followed everyone inside.

At first, the living room looked all right. Then they noticed a small lamp and a candy dish lying on the floor.

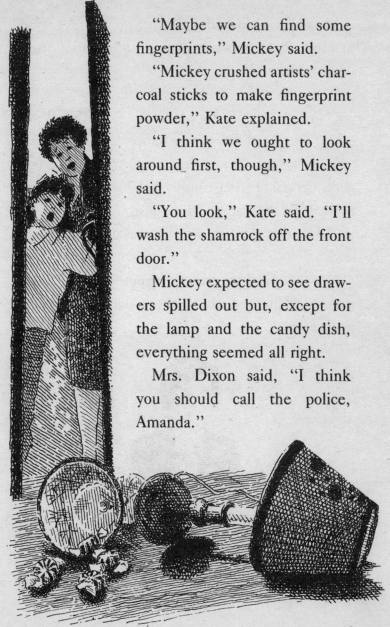

"Maybe we can find some fingerprints," Mickey said.

"Mickey crushed artists' charcoal sticks to make fingerprint powder," Kate explained.

"I think we ought to look around first, though," Mickey said.

"You look," Kate said. "I'll wash the shamrock off the front door."

Mickey expected to see drawers spilled out but, except for the lamp and the candy dish, everything seemed all right.

Mrs. Dixon said, "I think you should call the police, Amanda."

Miss Wink blushed. "Please, no. I don't want to admit that I was silly enough to leave my front door unlocked."

"Are you sure?" Mrs. Dixon said.

"Nothing seems to be missing," Miss Wink said. "Let's just forget this happened."

Mickey said, "I'm going to try to get some fingerprints from the candy dish, anyway." She headed for the back of the house.

"She's dying to try the charcoal powder," Kate said.

"Don't spill any on the carpet," Mrs. Dixon warned. "Charcoal will be worse than poster paint to clean up."

3

The Green Shamrock Gang

When Mickey saw the sign over the clubhouse door, she couldn't even think about fingerprints. Someone had printed "The Green Shamrock Gang Was Here," below the "Members Only" warning. The uneven green letters squiggled downhill.

"I wonder who the Green Shamrock Gang is," Kate said.

Mickey thought that her sister could be very dumb at times. "They're the ones who painted the green shamrock on Miss Wink's front door," she said.

"I know that," Kate said. "But who *are* they?"

"That's what we have to find out," Mickey said. She went into the shed.

Her books on how to be a detective were arranged on a long shelf. Kate's science books were on another shelf. On the bench below the shelves was a jar with the charcoal powder Mickey had made.

Everything seemed the same as when they had left. Or was it?

The charcoal sticks and stone she had used for making the powder were at one end of the bench. The stool she had been sitting on when she crushed the charcoal was near the door. When she looked up, green letters over the door warned, "The Banshee will get you."

"Kate, do you know what a banshee is?" Mickey asked.

"Some sort of Irish ghost, I think."

"Well, let's see if this banshee has fingerprints." Mickey took a small soft brush and dipped it in the charcoal powder. Then she went back outside. Standing on tiptoe, she could just reach the sign. It would be over the head of the small shamrock painter, unless he stood on the stool.

She dusted the powder on the sign. Two small black fingerprints appeared.

Kate said, "Now if we only knew whose prints they were."

"We'll find out," Mickey said. She put the

The Green Shamrock Scientific Detective Club MEMBERS ONLY

brush back on the bench.

Kate had a thought. "I'll bet Billy Wade is in the gang." Billy Wade was always causing trouble.

Mickey shook her head. "Billy wouldn't use paint that could be washed off," she said. "Remember when he daubed orange spots on the kindergarten turtles? Mrs. Collins never got the paint off the turtle shells."

Billy Wade and the turtles made Mickey remember something Uncle Corwin had told her. Their uncle Corwin was the chief of police on Indian Island. He had taught her a lot about detective work.

"That's another thing we'll need," she said.

"Turtles?" Kate asked. She had always wanted a pet, but they weren't allowed in the apartment building.

"Not turtles," Mickey said. "A file of criminals and their M.O.'s."

"M.O.?" Kate looked puzzled.

"M.O. — short for modus operandi."

"What's that?" Kate asked.

"I don't exactly know. But all police departments have files of M.O.'s. A crook does the same thing again and again. That's his M.O. If you know that, you know who did it." Mickey laughed. "Billy's M.O. is paint that won't wash off."

She picked up the pencil and was writing M. — when Miss Wink's scream interrupted her. "Cork is gone!"

Mickey dropped the pencil and headed for the house.

Kate knew that kittens sometimes climbed trees and couldn't get down.

"I'll look for Cork out here," she called. "If Miss Wink forgot to lock her house, she might have forgotten to close the basement door, too."

"Good thinking," Mickey said.

As usual, Miss Wink was mixed up. The tan kitten was on top of the refrigerator licking her paws. Kilkenny, the kitten with an upside down W on his forehead, was missing.

"*That's* Cork," Mickey said.

"Oh," Miss Wink said. "Everything was so muddled this morning. I didn't really look at the kittens."

"You're sure you shut them in the basement?"

Miss Wink's head bobbed up and down. "I'm positive of that. I distinctly heard them mewing and scratching behind the door."

Mickey thought that the Green Shamrock Gang probably heard the kittens and let them out. She thought of something else, too.

"Maybe the kittens knocked over the lamp," she said. "The noise could have scared Kilkenny."

"Mickey's right," her mother said. "He might just be hiding in the house."

"Oh, I hope so," Miss Wink said.

While Kate searched the yard, Miss Wink, Mrs. Dixon, and Mickey searched the house.

Kilkenny was nowhere to be found.

4

Where Do We Start?

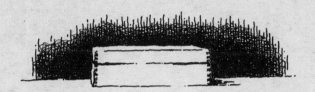

When Mickey came back, Kate was still looking for the cat. "I haven't found Cork out here," she said.

"Not Cork," Mickey said. "Kilkenny. Miss Wink didn't know the difference."

Kate said, "We ought to organize a search party."

"Great idea — if we could find anyone to search," Mickey said. "They're all probably down at the St. Patrick's Day Parade."

Kate said, "Not the Green Shamrock Gang."

Mickey nodded. "And we have to find *them* first. If they took Kilkenny, they may still have him. And if they let him get away, they ought to help look for him."

"Where do we start?" Kate asked.

"Let's think for a minute. Why call themselves the Green Shamrock Gang?"

"That's easy," Kate said. "Because it's St. Patrick's Day."

Mickey smiled and nodded. "Exactly. If there were a real Green Shamrock Gang, we would have heard of them."

Kate said, "Maybe it's a new gang."

Mickey wasn't listening. She was thinking about the Green Shamrock name.

"That's it!" Mickey cried, jumping up.

"They're new?" Kate said.

"There is no gang," Mickey explained. "Someone only pretended that there was."

"Well . . . maybe." Kate sounded doubtful.

"We're looking for a boy or girl, someone who isn't very tall and needed the stool to write on our sign."

"How do we find him — or her?" Then, because she still wasn't sure it was one person, she added, "Or them?"

"We interview the witnesses," Mickey said.

"There were no witnesses," Kate said.

Mickey ignored her. "We'll start with Mr. Swensen."

Mr. Swensen had a small store around the corner from their school.

"Why Mr. Swensen?" Kate asked.

"Honestly, Kate. Who knows everyone and everything in this neighborhood?"

"Mr. Swensen."

"I'll get the list I made of things we need for the detective club," Mickey said.

"*Scientific* detective club," Kate said firmly. Then she added, "Why take the list?"

"We can't just go in and ask questions. We have to buy something."

"Good thing we got our allowances this morning," Kate said.

"We have more than that," Mickey said. "Mr. Wink gave us five dollars for our club treasury, remember."

Suddenly both girls had the same thought. They ran into the clubhouse. The five dollar bill had been in a wooden box on the bench. Now it was gone.

Inside the box they saw a note that said, "I owe you $5." It was signed with a small green shamrock.

Kate said, "I guess the first thing we need to buy is a padlock for the clubhouse door."

5

Clues and Deductions

Mickey studied the note. "Another clue," she announced. "What does it tell us?"

Kate said, "Our money was taken by the Green Shamrock Gang."

"What else?" Mickey asked.

Kate stared at the note. Like the green letters on the clubhouse sign, the letters were wavery and uneven.

"Someone isn't very good at printing," she said.

"Right," Mickey said. "*Someone*. This proves there isn't any Green Shamrock Gang."

"I don't see why," Kate said.

Mickey grinned. " '*I* owe you.' Not '*we* owe you.' It's one person pretending to be a gang."

"A single person might be harder to find than a whole gang," Kate said.

"Think about what we know," Mickey said.

Kate thought. "He or she is very short and doesn't print very good." Quickly she added, "Maybe someone in first grade."

"That's why we have to talk to Mr. Swensen. All the kids buy candy from him."

"No one would be dumb enough to spend the whole five dollars on candy or talk about where the money came from if he did."

Mickey said, "A lot of criminals talk about what they've done. Uncle Corwin said that's often how they get caught."

"You think this green shamrock person will brag to Mr. Swensen about painting Miss Wink's door?"

"I don't know," Mickey said. "But do you have a better place to start?"

Kate didn't.

6

What Mr. Swensen Knew

Mr. Swensen's store had been on the corner of Wells and Hawthorne for as long as anyone could remember. He sold school supplies and other items that people in the neighborhood might need.

The store had a candy counter that was higher than Kate's head. Even though Mr. Swensen cleaned it every day, the glass was always smudged with small handprints. No matter what he said, children leaned against it while trying to decide what to buy. There were so many things — licorice whips, bubble gum, lemon drops, pink dots — that deciding took a long time.

The twins walked past the candy to where Mr. Swensen was piling soup cans on a shelf.

"Hello, girls," he said. "Parade over?"

Kate said, "No. We went to the airport with the Winks."

Mr. Swensen smiled. "That's right. Horace did say he was leaving today." Horace and Mr. Swensen had been friends since grade school.

"For all the customers I've had, I could have gone to the airport, too," Mr. Swensen said.

That was bad news for the store, Mickey thought, but good news for solving the mystery. With few customers, he would remember Green Shamrock.

He said, "Everyone has gone downtown for the St. Patrick's Day Parade, I guess."

Kate started to say, "Not every —" but Mickey frowned and the look stopped her sister in mid-sentence.

"No candy business?" Mickey asked.

Mr. Swensen shook his head. "Only thing I sold all morning was three cans of cat food."

Mickey's heart began to thump. "I didn't know you sold cat food," she said.

"Usually don't. Most people buy it at the super-market. I keep some around, though, just as I keep milk and toothpaste. You would be surprised at the people who go to the supermarket and forget milk. They should make a list."

Mickey said, "We have a list." She handed it
to him.

"Let's see," he said. "I have sandwich bags.
And the chalk. No tape measure, unless you want
the cloth ones that are back with the sewing
things."

"What about padlocks?" Kate asked.

"Nope. Try a hardware store." Mr. Swensen

looked up from the list. "Why do you want all this stuff?"

Mickey said, "We're setting up a detective club in Miss Wink's old shed."

"A *scientific* detective club," Kate added.

"Sounds like fun." Mr. Swensen winked. "Can I join?"

Mickey knew he was teasing them. It was the opportunity she wanted, though.

"You could help us practice to be detectives," she said.

"How?"

"I'll pretend to be Sherlock Holmes and tell you about the cat food buyer. You tell me if I'm right."

She paused and closed her eyes as if she were thinking.

"The person was little, maybe only in first grade, and paid for the cat food with a five dollar bill." Mickey opened her eyes again.

"Very good," Mr. Swensen said. He seemed impressed. "Tell me who it was."

Kate said, "We don't know. You tell us."

"I don't know either," Mr. Swensen said.

"You mean it was someone who doesn't live around here?" Mickey asked.

"I mean he's new in the neighborhood. Told me his family was moving in today."

When he said that, both girls remembered the moving van that was parked outside of their building.

"Nice little boy, maybe five or six, with a cute little gray kitten," Mr. Swensen said.

Mickey headed for the door. "We'll be back later," she called, and ran outside.

Kate thought she should explain why they were in a hurry, but she didn't know what to say. Besides, she was interested in the moving van, too.

"Goodbye," she shouted, dashing after her sister.

7

Kilkenny and Friend

The moving van was gone. The front door of their apartment building was still propped open, though.

"That's strange," Mickey said.

"Why?" Kate asked. "The Abbotts moved out last week."

"Why would the boy take Kilkenny?" Mickey said. "No one in this building is allowed to have pets."

"If he just moved in, he might not know that."

Mickey went into the front hall and looked at the row of mailboxes. Sure enough, the box that used to say Abbott now had a new name: Dr. and Mrs. O'Brien.

Kate said, "I wouldn't think that Dr. O'Brien,

whoever he is, would let a small boy wander alone around a new neighborhood."

"Perhaps no one knew," Mickey said. "You remember what moving day is like. They might not even have noticed that he was gone."

Kate said, "Let's go upstairs and ask about Kilkenny."

"You don't just ask someone if he's guilty of kitten-stealing," Mickey said. "Not without proof."

"We don't have any proof," Kate said.

"Sure we do. The note he left in the wooden box. Come on."

"Where?" Kate asked.

"To get the note, of course!" Mickey explained.

When they got to Miss Wink's back yard, Kate said, "I thought we left the clubhouse door open."

"We did."

The shed door was now closed.

"Shhh," Mickey whispered. She yanked the door open.

A small blond boy stood next to the bench. Even for a first-grader he was short.

The boy had the top of the wooden box in his hand. Next to the box, Kilkenny was eating out of an open can of cat food. Two other cans were stacked on the bench.

The boy turned around and his eyes widened.

"Aha!" Mickey shouted. "We caught you!"

"Wha . . . what do you want?" he asked.

Mickey said, "The question is, what do *you* want?"

"I was returning the change." His lips trembled. "I'll pay back the rest of the money in a couple of weeks. I promise. Only, please, don't tell my father."

Kate thought he didn't look like a thief. He looked like a frightened little boy. She held out her hand to him.

"I'm Kate Dixon," she said. "This is my sister Mickey. You just moved in downstairs of us, didn't you?"

The boy backed away, and Mickey glared.

Then she saw tears in the boy's eyes. Real villains never cried.

"We won't have you arrested," Mickey said. Still the boy seemed afraid.

"Don't tell my father," he repeated.

"We won't," Kate said.

"What's your name?" Mickey asked.

"Joseph O'Brien," he said. "Joey."

Kate said, "It was kind of you to feed Kilkenny."

"Kilkenny," Joey said. He almost smiled. "I wondered what his name was. What's the other one called?"

"Cork," Kate said.

"Neat," Joey said. Then he seemed to remember what he had done. His lip trembled. "I *will* pay you back, honest."

"You'd better," Mickey warned. She tried to sound stern. "We should take Kilkenny inside. Miss Wink is very worried."

Mickey picked up the kitten. Joey picked up the open can of cat food.

Kate looked in the wooden box. Inside were three dollar bills, some coins, and a new note. It said, "I owe you 167 pennies."

Joey O'Brien was a strange little boy.

8
Joey Explains

When Miss Wink saw Kilkenny, she gave a little squeal. Mickey handed the kitten to her.

"Oh, kitty," she said. "They found you."

Kilkenny stuck out his small pink tongue and licked Miss Wink's hand as she put him down.

"*I* found him," Joey declared.

"After you let him loose," Mickey said.

"I didn't mean to. They were climbing around in the living room and —"

"But I locked them in the basement," Miss Wink said.

Mickey closed the basement door. Then she pulled on the handle. The door swung open.

"You *thought* you locked them in the basement," she said. "The latch doesn't catch."

Miss Wink stared at the open door. "I never noticed that."

"The kittens must have pushed the door open," Mickey said. "You told us they were scratching on it."

Joey said, "The front door wasn't closed tight either, and when I drew the shamrock —" He stopped abruptly. He looked scared again. "I . . . I let the kittens out by accident. Cork came right back, but I had a hard time finding Kilkenny."

On cue, the gray kitten came out from under the kitchen table.

"Oh, look," Miss Wink said. "Kilkenny knows his name already."

Kilkenny rubbed against Joey's ankles.

Kate said, "I think it's Joey that the kitten knows."

The boy reached down and stroked the cat's neck.

"It took me a long time to find him," Joey said. "When I did, he seemed hungry. I thought there might be cat food in the shed. Instead, I found the money and went to buy some." The words came very fast. "I'll pay it back," he promised again.

Kate said, "We believe you, Joey."

"Forget the money for now," Mickey said. "Why did you paint the shamrock? And our sign?"

His lip started trembling.

"I was in the way when my mom was unpacking so I went and sat on the front step of the building. The moving men said I was in the way there, too. They told me to stop bothering them and go to the St. Patrick's Day Parade."

He took a breath and frowned as if trying to think of a way to explain. "I've never been to a parade. When I asked my father if I could go, he said I was too little to be there alone." He lifted his chin to make himself seem taller. "I'm in third grade."

"Third grade!" Kate couldn't believe it. "How old are you?"

Joey smiled and his whole face lit up. "Six," he said proudly. "I'm gifted. That's what my father says. He teaches college and he knows a lot. We moved to Springvale because they have a good program for kids like me."

Tears filled Joey's eyes again.

"I didn't want to move. I mean, where I was, they were used to me. I didn't have any friends, but at least they didn't make fun of me anymore."

Kate said, "I've never known anyone who was gifted."

"It's nothing special," he said, then grinned. "My parents started teaching me Latin and arithmetic when I was two years old."

Mickey asked, "Do you know what modus operandi is?"

"Sure. In Latin, it means manner of working."

"And what's a banshee?" Kate asked.

"She's the Irish lady of death — a spirit who is supposed to come when someone is going to die."

Joey's face was very serious again.

Kate wondered if all gifted people went from sad to happy and back to sad so quickly.

"You still haven't told me why you painted the shamrock on my door," Miss Wink said.

"I . . . I guess after I went behind the apartment building and saw the shed, I got mad at everyone."

"Why did that make you mad?" Mickey asked.

"The sign said Members Only. Springvale was going to be just like the last place we lived, where no one would let me do things with them."

Joey did the lip trembling thing again and tears began to roll down his cheeks. "My f-f-father promised I could have a pet this year," he said. "Now I can't."

Miss Wink said, "You could have Kilkenny. He likes you, and I don't need two kittens."

"Pets aren't allowed in the apartment building."

"That's all right," Miss Wink said. "Kilkenny can stay here with me, but he'll be yours."

Kate was surprised. Miss Wink sounded so . . . so sensible.

Mickey surprised her even more.

"If we asked them, would your parents let you go to the parade with us?"

"I don't know," Joey said. "I mean, you're not old enough to babysit, are you?"

Miss Wink said, "I'm old enough and I think it might be fun to go to the parade. Why don't we ask if you could go with me?"

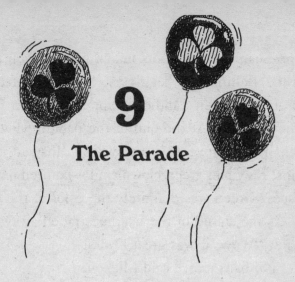

9

The Parade

The O'Briens seemed very pleasant, not stuffy the way Kate expected a college professor and his wife might be.

"So you're the twins," Dr. O'Brien said. "We just met your mother. And you must be Amanda Wink from next door."

Miss Wink nodded and smiled. "We were wondering if Joey could go with us to see the St. Patrick's Day Parade."

"How nice of you to offer," Mrs. O'Brien said.

"It will be all right, then?" Joey said.

"Yes," Dr. O'Brien said. "It will be all right."

"Wowee! Let's go!" Joey shouted.

By the time they got to Bayfront Drive, the parade was almost over. They were barely in time to see the Shannon Bagpipers march past in their green kilts. Behind the bagpipers, boys in leprechaun costumes threw candies wrapped in green foil to the children. At the end of the parade, clowns in small cars drove past and waved. Instead of red lips, they had green clown smiles painted on their faces. Green was definitely the color of the day.

As the sound of the bagpipes faded away, Joey said, "Wow, it was great."

"No banshees," said Mickey.

"No," said Joey. His grin seemed to cover his whole face. "My first parade and my first pet all in one day." Then he looked up at Miss Wink. "Can Kilkenny really be my kitten?"

"Of course," she said.

"You could be in our scientific detective club, too," Mickey said. "A gifted member might be very helpful."

Joey's grin got even wider. "Honest?" he asked.

"Honest," Kate and Mickey said at the same time.